1,400 pounds of evil.

The bull whirled around and started trotting away from the herd. Well, that had been easy enough, and I figgered this might be a good time for me to install my Anti-Bull Procedures. Barking at the top of my lungs, I rushed past the horse and sank my teeth into the left rear hock of this large but cowardly...

One detail a guy tends to forget about these bulls is that, while they're very large and appear to be slow and dim-witted, they're actually none of those things except large. I mean, it's hard to believe that a bull weighing in at 1,300 or 1,400 pounds can turn on a dime and give you the change.

But they can. And he did.

The Case of the Hooking Bull

John R. Erickson

Illustrations by Gerald L. Holmes

Puffin Books

*This book is dedicated to the cowboys
I have known and ridden with over the years—
the Jim Streeters, the Jake Parkers, and
the Frankie McWhorters who have shared their
wisdom and knowledge with me.*

PUFFIN BOOKS
Published by the Penguin Group
Penguin Putnam Books for Young Readers,
345 Hudson Street, New York, New York 10014, U.S.A.
Penguin Books Ltd, 27 Wrights Lane, London W8 5TZ, England
Penguin Books Australia Ltd, Ringwood, Victoria, Australia
Penguin Books Canada Ltd, 10 Alcorn Avenue, Toronto, Ontario, Canada M4V 3B2
Penguin Books (N.Z.) Ltd, 182-190 Wairau Road, Auckland 10, New Zealand

Penguin Books Ltd, Registered Offices:
Harmondsworth, Middlesex, England

First published in the United States of America
by Maverick Books, Gulf Publishing Company, 1992
Published by Puffin Books, a member of
Penguin Putnam Books for Young Readers, 1999

13 15 17 19 20 18 16 14 12

LIBRARY OF CONGRESS CATALOGING-IN-PUBLICATION DATA
Erickson, John R., date
The case of the hooking bull / John R. Erickson ; illustrations by Gerald L. Holmes.
p. cm.
Previously published: Houston, Tex. : Gulf Pub. Co., c1992. (Hank the Cowdog ; 18)
Summary: Unsupervised for the day, Hank the cowdog and his human friends,
Little Alfred and Slim Chance, mind the ranch with humorous results.
ISBN 0-14-130394-8 (pbk.)
[1. Dogs Fiction. 2. Ranch life—West (U.S.) Fiction. 3. West (U.S.) Fiction.
4. Humorous stories.]
I. Holmes, Gerald L., ill. II. Title. III. Series: Erickson, John R., date
Hank the Cowdog ; #18
[PZ7.E72556Catf 1999] [Fic]—dc21 99-19584 CIP

Printed in the United States of America

CONTENTS

CHAPTER ONE

Watering the Shrubbery

It's me again, Hank the Cowdog. It started out to be a normal summertime day. Drover and I were asleep on our gunnysack beds under the gas tanks, although I wasn't entirely asleep.

Very seldom do I indulge myself in 100 percent sleep because . . . well, just think about it. There's no telling who or what might come onto the ranch and do who-knows-what.

Let us say that I was in a light doze, listening to Drover grunt, wheeze, and snore in his sleep. Perhaps I had a few matters of business on my mind, but not many, and for sure I wasn't thinking about the Huge Horrible Hooking Bull in the north pasture.

Maybe I should have been, because before the

day was over, that monster of a bull would . . . better not reveal any more of the story. I'd hate to scare the kids too badly too soon.

This bull belonged to the neighbors, see, and he'd been tearing down gates and fences and causing a lot of trouble. Slim and Loper had run him out of the pasture three or four times, but he kept coming back and destroying fences.

You probably know how much your average cowboy enjoys repairing fence in the heat of summer.

Not much. By the second or third time, he starts thinking of naughty things to do to the party who is destroying the fence.

But doing naughty things to such a big, mean, huge horned creature isn't as easy as you might think. The problem comes from the fact that bulls are pretty good hands at fighting back.

Oops, I wasn't going to reveal any more.

Yes, this is going to be a pretty scary story, so use your own judgment. If you have a weak nervous system, you might ought to find something else to do and leave this story alone.

Where was I? Oh yes, under the gas tanks. I leaped to my feet and took a deep, luxurious stretch. I was about to kick Drover awake and outline the day's work when I heard the screen door slam up at the house.

Drover heard it too. His ears jumped, his eyes popped open, and he yelled, "Scraps!" And in a flash he was gone.

"Drover, wait! Come back here."

He came padding back. "What's wrong?"

"What's wrong is that you cheated. Do you think it's fair for you to leave while I'm in the middle of a stretch?"

"Well . . ."

"Of course it's not. That's the kind of shabby trick I would expect from Pete, but I'm shocked that you'd try such a thing."

"Well . . ."

"If we can't play fair, Drover, we shouldn't play at all."

"I guess not, but I was hungry."

"Everyone's hungry, Drover, but the kind of hunger we need in this world is a hunger for fair play and manners."

"I guess so."

"Are you ashamed of yourself?"

"Well . . . I guess so. I've always wanted to be a good dog."

"I know you have, son, and I know you will be." I gave him a pat on the shoulder to make him feel better. "Now, we'll start this thing all over again and do it right this time. On the count of four, you may race up to the yard gate."

"Four?"

"That's correct."

"I thought everybody started on the count of three."

"I will leave on three. You will leave on four. That way you won't be tempted to cheat again."

"Oh good. Thanks, Hank."

"Any time, Drover, any time."

I was the first to reach the yard gate, heh-heh.

There I found . . . hmm . . . no scraps, but the gate was open. Leaving the yard gate open was a transgression of Sally May's Law, and I could think of only one party on the ranch who might do such a thing.

Hint: He was five years old, walked on two legs, made lots of noise, and often had mischief on his mind. If you guessed Junior the Buzzard or Slim Chance, the cowboy, you're wrong. The correct answer is Little Alfred.

Yes, Little Alfred was bad about leaving gates open, and I had a hunch that this was some of his work. I confirmed this hunch by subjugating the area around the gate to a Sniffatory Analysis.

I don't want to scare anybody with these big technical terms. A Sniffatory Analysis means pretty muchly the same as "checking the area for scent," but those of us in the Security Business, and I'm talking about those of us who live with it day and night, tend to refer to things in heavy-duty technical terms.

I mean, it's just second nature to us, and I guess we forget that most of the world doesn't understand big scientific words. I'll try to keep it as simple as possible, but you must bear in mind that . . .

All at once this seems a little boring.

Okay, where were we? Yard gate, that's where we were. I had just run an S.A. of the area around the yard gate, and, yes, it turned up positive for Little Alfred. The little stinkpot was running loose, and since I couldn't hear him making the sounds of bulldozers or dynamite, I suspected that he was up to no good.

I crept up the hill and checked it out. Ah yes, there he was, roping chickens in front of the machine shed. That was good clean entertainment for the boy. Roping cats might have been even better, but I noticed that Pete was nowhere in sight.

Pete was no mountain of intelligence, but he had figgered out that rope business. The moment Little Alfred stepped out the door with a loaded rope in his hands, Kitty-Kitty tended to vanish.

And somehow the world always seemed a better, brighter place when Pete disappeared.

Well, the boy was busy and happy roping chickens, so I went back down to the yard gate to run a more thorough search for scraps. It was then that I heard Drover's voice.

"Hank, have you counted to four yet?"

"Not yet, son. We're at 3.5 and holding. Just be patient."

"I'll try, but I sure could use some scraps."

"I understand, Drover, but we mustn't jump the count. The entire universe is like a giant clock, with mathematics as its spring. If we ignore the numbers, there's no telling what might happen."

"What?"

"No!"

I sniffed out the ground just outside the gate. Nothing, not a single trace of eggs, bacon, or even burned toast. For a moment I considered going through the gate into Forbidden Territory—into Sally May's yard, in other words—but I was well aware that dogs weren't allowed there. I was also very much aware of the consequences of getting . . .

On the other hand, she was nowhere in sight, and Little Alfred just might have left a few juicy morsels of breakfast scraps within the fence, and rather than run the risk of letting Pete devour all the scraps, I decided to make a small penetration of the yard.

My front paws crossed the line. I waited and watched. No sign of Sally May or her broom. I moved forward, causing my hind paws to cross into the Danger Zone. Still no sign of Sally May.

Well, this could mean only one thing. She had softened her position on Dogs in the Yard and had finally realized that a yard with dogs is a safer yard.

A happier yard. A better yard in every way. And it's true. A yard without a dog is like a house without a home.

Well, now that she had come to her senses on that score, I felt as though a heavy burden had been lifted off of my soldiers. Instead of creeping and cringing, cowering and crouching, flinching at every little sound for fear that I might be thrashed with a broom, I loosened up and began to enjoy my new freedom.

I was SO proud of Sally May for working out a compromise on the yard business. I mean, even your bigger and tougher breeds of dog can admire a nice, well-kept yard, with its mowed grass, edged edges, neat little patches of flowers here and there, shrubbery . . .

And speaking of shrubbery, I passed one of her shrubberies and noticed that it had never been marked. Can you imagine that? This poor little shrubbery had been on the ranch for . . . what? Two years? Three? A long time, and it had never been marked.

The poor, lonely little shrubbery! Well, you know me. As long as I have an ounce of strength and an ounce of fluid left in my body, I'll be glad to share it with a shrubbery, and I did. And just to be sure that Pete got the message, I gave it two coats.

"LEAVE MY SHRUBS ALONE, YOU NASTY DOG!! SCAT!"

Huh?

The voice sounded a lot like Sally May's, and when the first rock bounced off my ribs . . . OOF! . . . I was almost sure that it was . . . OOF! . . . Sally May speaking.

You see, she kept a small pile of rocks beside the back door, almost as though she had planned all along to use them on, well, stray dogs or someone who had penetrated the sanctimony of her precious yard.

What we had here was a simple case of mistaken identity, and rather than run the risk of further confusion, I ran for my life and moved my business underneath the car, which was parked just beyond the yard gate.

From this vantage point, I peeked out at the field of battle and noticed that . . . hmmm. Slim and Loper had joined her on the back porch.

Slim was loaded down with suitcases. Loper was carrying Baby Molly, a diaper bag, and a fold-up high chair.

It appeared that someone was leaving the ranch.

CHAPTER TWO

Code Name
"Abilene"

From my bunker position, I homed in on their voice frequencies and picked up these bits of information:

1. Sally May and Loper were going to Abilene to attend the wedding of . . . someone. Two people. Two people were getting married—a man and a woman.

2. One of the alleged persons-to-be-wed was Sally May's cousin.

3. It appeared that Loper had resisted the idea of attending the wedding, arguing that he had a month's work to do on the ranch and no hope of getting caught up.

4. To which Sally May replied: "If it was a team roping, a rodeo, or a dog fight, you'd be caught up

in a New York minute, but when it comes to my kinfolks, you always seem to be snowed under!"

5. Loper seemed to have no answer to that. He scowled up at the clouds and tugged at his necktie and mumbled, "This thing's choking me to death. I'll have brain damage before we reach Guthrie."

6. Slim wore his everyday cowboy clothes and a big smile. I got the feeling that he was enjoying all of this.

7. Sally May pointed out that wearing a tie once or twice a year wouldn't kill Loper, and even if it did, she "just might enjoy the insurance money"—whatever that meant.

8. Slim laughed out loud. Loper glared at him and his lips formed words I couldn't hear.

So there you are. Those were the clues I amassed from my observation point beneath the car. Pretty impressive, huh? You bet it was.

Oh yes, one last detail.

All at once Baby Molly began to cry. Loper bounced her around in his arms, then handed her over to Sally May. "Here, Ma, your daughter's calling you."

Sally May took the baby and got her settled down. Then she turned a pair of steely eyes on Slim. "Slim, I'll be honest. I have some misgivings about leaving you in charge of my house and child."

He nodded. "Yes ma'am, I can understand that, sure can."

"You *will* feed my child something while I'm gone, won't you?"

"Oh yes ma'am."

"Vegetables?"

"You bet, lots of vegetables."

"He needs to take a bath tonight and brush his teeth after every meal."

"You bet."

"At bedtime, I usually read him a story."

"Uh-huh."

"And then I tuck him in and we say our prayers."

"Yalp."

"Sometimes he wants a glass of juice at bed-time."

"Uh-huh."

"So if you want to make him a glass of orange juice, that will be fine."

"Okay, orange juice."

"Slim, can you remember all this?"

"Oh yeah, you bet."

"Maybe I should make a list."

Loper eased her down the sidewalk toward the car. "Everything'll be fine, hon. Old Slim might not look very smart, but he's really pretty stupid."

"This is no time for joking."

"Sally May, we'll only be gone for two days."

"Pompeii was destroyed in fifteen minutes."

"Hon, Slim can't even find his hip pocket in fifteen minutes."

"I'm not feeling any better."

"Shall we go or shall we stay home?"

By this time they were standing right beside the car. Their feet, ankles, etc. were only a matter of inches away from my nose. Sally May was wearing a dress, don't you see, which meant that her ankles were sort of bare.

For some strange reason . . . it was just an impulse, see, a sudden impulse that happened before I could think about it . . . all at once it occurred to me that I should, well, lick Sally May on the ankle, you might say.

Maybe she hadn't seen me under the car and maybe she wasn't expecting anyone to lick her on the ankle, because she sure took it the wrong way.

"AAAAAAAAAAAAAAAA!!"

Yes, I'm almost sure it caught her by surprise, the way she jumped back and kicked the car door all in one rapid motion. It appeared to hurt her foot, but the good news was that she missed my nose.

"What's wrong, hon?"

"Something licked me on the ankle, and I have a pretty good idea who it was." Her face appeared upside down in the little slot of daylight between the car and the ground.

I, uh, whapped my tail several times upon the, uh, gravel drive and tried to squeeze up a big, friendly cowdog smile, as if to say, "Oh, I guess that was, uh, your ankle, right?"

"STOP LICKING ME! I have to go to a wedding this afternoon and I don't want to smell like a sewer!"

Okay, fine. If that's the way she felt about it, by George, I would just pack up my licks and take them somewhere else. But she didn't need to screech at me like that.

Dogs have feelings too.

In many ways, we're very sensitive, and all that screeching and yelling and so forth has a dilapidating effect on our . . . something. Inner being, I guess.

So after having my inner being smashed and crushed, I crawled out from under the car and went slinking off with my tail between my legs and sat down beside the fence, some ten yards away from Sally May, and proceeded to beam hurtful looks at her.

She didn't notice the hurtful looks. Instead, she turned to Slim and said, "And speaking of dogs, I don't want any dogs in my yard while I'm gone."

"Yes ma'am."

"And I don't suppose we need to discuss dogs in the house."

Slim shifted his weight to his other leg. "Now, I'm pretty strict on that, Sally May. These dogs don't get away with much around me, they sure don't."

Sally May took a deep, slow breath. "This is

probably a mistake. I'll probably regret this for the rest of my life, but if we're going to make the wedding, we'd better go."

Loper turned to Slim. "Can you run that bull out by yourself or would you rather wait until I get back?"

Slim smiled. "One riot, one Ranger."

"Well, watch him. He's big enough to hurt somebody."

"So am I."

Loper opened the back door and started pitching luggage inside. Sally May called Little Alfred away from his chicken roping, and he came down the hill for the Final Ceremonies.

Holding the baby in the curve of her left arm, she bent down and hugged the boy with her right. "Alfred, I want you to promise me that you'll be a good boy while Mommy's gone."

"I pwomise."

"And that you won't do anything Mommy wouldn't want you to do."

"I pwomise."

"Mommy will miss you and . . ." So forth.

I've reported only part of the conversation between Sally May and Alfred. It went on for quite a spell and I quit listening to it. You see, my attention had been drawn to a small detail that a lot of dogs would have overlooked.

It suddenly dawned on me that after packing the luggage into the back seat, *Loper had left the car door open*. Everything in this old world has a reason. A car-door-left-open is part and partial of this old world, therefore it has a reason.

It was my job to find the reason. In other words, why had Loper, a careful and precise kind of feller, left that door open? To air out the car? No. To load Baby Molly into the back with the luggage? No. To let Sally May ride in the . . . no.

I submitted this mystery to the Funnel of Logic (another of the techniques we use in the Security Business) and it funneled down to one and only one simple explanation: For private and unknown reasons, Loper wanted ME to accompany them on their trip to Abilene, and possibly even to attend the wedding.

Why? I had no idea. The Funnel of Logic does not address why-questions. It only deals with broad general truths and long-term trends.

Well, a trip to Abilene wasn't exactly part of my scheduling for the next couple of days. Could I squeeze it in? For anyone else, the answer would have been a big, lymphatic NO. I had much too much work lined up to be running all over the state of Texas.

But for Loper and Sally May? You bet. Loyalty runs deep in my line of cowdogs. When duty calls, we are there, Johnny-on-the-Spot.

It happened that Drover appeared at that very moment and said, "Hi Hank, I got bored."

"Never mind what you got, Drover. I have been called out on an assignment. Within minutes, I'll be leaving on a secret mission."

"I'll be derned. Where you going?"

I glanced over both shoulders and dropped my voice to a whisper. "We're not sure, Drover. The decoy destination is Abilene. The actual destination could be anywhere: London, Paris, Bangkok, Amarillo. A guy never knows."

"Sounds pretty exciting."

"Exactly. While I'm gone, you'll be in charge."

"Oops."

"I know, but we must take life as it really is. Take care of things, son. Good-bye."

Before this emotional parting could get out of hand, I turned away, squared my shoulders, lifted my head to a stern angle, and marched to the transport vehicle, which was waiting for me.

I hopped in, found myself a place on the seat amidst the suitcases and high chair, and settled down for a long . . .

Perhaps I had misread the signals.

The, uh, secret mission was suddenly cancelled, so to speak.

After thinking it over, Loper must have decided that . . . well, just think about the risks of . . .

I stayed at the ranch, and never mind the details.

CHAPTER THREE

Emerald Pond

As they pulled away from the house, Slim and Little Alfred waved good-bye, and I found myself standing beside Drover again.

"That was a pretty short trip."

I gave him a wilting glare. "My orders were cancelled at the last moment."

"There for a second, I thought Loper was going to cancel *you*."

"That was your interpretation of your impression. The actual truth, Drover, often lies hidden beneath the facts."

"He looked pretty mad to me."

"Drover, I feel you're trying to make a mockery of my misfortune, almost as though you enjoyed watching me get dragged from the car and pitched into the weeds."

"Well . . . it did look pretty funny, I guess."

"There we are, a confession! That will go into my report."

"Oh drat."

"And in the meantime, let me share something with you."

"Thanks, Hank."

"You're welcome." I began pacing up and down in front of him, as I often do when I find myself tugging at deep and difficult concepts. "Drover, in the process of running this outfit and dealing with dim-witted employees, I've found that most situations can be improved when the higher authorities, such as myself, employ two simple words."

"I'll be derned."

"Just two words, Drover, simple words that have a magic effect."

"Don't tell me, let me guess." He rolled his eyes and set his lips into a peculiar shape. "Let's see. Happy birthday?"

"No."

"Merry Christmas?"

"Wrong again. You'll never guess it."

"Yes I will."

"That's three words."

"Yeah, I know, but it wasn't a guess."

"Oh."

"Thank you?"

"You're welcome."

"No, that was my guess: thank you."

"Of course. No, that's wrong too."

"I'm sorry?"

"That's okay, I didn't expect you to guess it."

"No, that was another guess."

"Are you trying to be funny?"

"Not really."

"Good, because this is not the time to be funny. Now, what was your last guess?"

"I'm sorry."

"I told you not to worry about it."

"Yeah, but that was my guess: I'm sorry."

"Yes, of course. No, that's wrong, and we're just about out of time. I will now tell you the two magic words that are most often used by efficient managers, bosses, top executives, generals, admirals, and Heads of Ranch Security."

He sat down and wagged his stub tail in the dust. "Oh good, I can hardly wait. What are they?"

I stopped pacing and whirled around, facing him with narrowed eyes and a worldly sneer. "The first is SHUT and the second is UP."

"Shut up?"

"That's correct. Keep those two words before

your eyes and near to your heart, Drover. Repeat them, memorize them, and the next time you think you've seen me in an embarrassing situation, pull them out of the vast garbage heap of your mind. And in the meantime, shut up."

"Okay, Hank, I think I've got it."

Well, getting the runt straightened out had taken longer than I had expected, but some jobs can't wait. Once the cat is out of the sandbox, you have to . . . I don't know, change the sand, I suppose.

Well, when Loper and Sally May drove out of sight, Slim yawned and checked the location of the sun. Then he looked down at Little Alfred and frowned.

"Well, Button, it's me and you against the world. Don't forget all them things your ma told you not to do, and in case she missed anything, you can just figger that the answer is no."

"Okay, Swim."

"I didn't hire onto this outfit as a baby-sitter, and don't you forget it."

"Okay, Swim."

"I'm too old and gripey and set in my ways to be puttin' up with a green colt like you." His gaze drifted over to me and Drover. I gave him a big smile, and he, well, appeared to curl his lip at me. "You and your two souphounds. I've got fifty-three jobs that need doin' and here I am, playin' bedpan nurse to the Three Stooges."

"We'll have fun, Swim."

"Huh. I have my doubts about that."

"Is it time to eat, Swim?"

"Eat! Good honk, son, your ma's dust has hardly settled and you're already wantin' to eat? How come you didn't eat yesterday?"

"I did but I'm hungwy again."

Slim growled and shook his head. "What do you want to eat?"

"Oh, wet's see. Ice cweam."

"No ice cream. Your ma gave me strict orders to give you nourishing feed, with plenty of vegetables. What kind of vegetables do you want with your Vienna sausage? How 'bout some canned peas?" Alfred shook his head. "Canned corn? That's pretty good stuff, that corn." Alfred shook his head. "All right, then stewed tomaters."

Alfred made a sour face. "I don't wike stewed dummaters."

"Well, you're too hard to please. I ain't runnin' a short-order house for fussy eaters. How 'bout some ketchup?"

"Okay, Swim, I wike ketchup."

"Then that settles it." Slim hitched up his pants. "I'll fix us a bait of Vienna sausage, with a side order of ketchup. And crackers. We'll break out some crackers. Now, that's a real gen-u-wine cowboy dinner."

"And then we'll have some ice cweam."

"No, and then we WON'T have some ice cream. I don't want your ma tellin' the neighbors that I corrupted her child with junk food." Slim yawned and stretched. "Boy, this heat makes me as loggy as a fat pup. Button, we may be forced to shut down the ranch and take ourselves a little nap after a bit."

"Aw Swim! I don't want to take a nap."

Slim bent over and looked the boy right in the eyes. "Yeah, but you WILL take a nap, 'cause I'm going to take a nap and I ain't about to close my eyes while you're running a-loose."

"Okay, Swim, I'll take a nap."

"That's more like it. I hate to be stern and cruel, but rules is rules, and law is law. Let's go to the house."

Slim yawned again and started toward the back door. Little Alfred gave me a wink and a smile, and he whispered, "I'll be out to pway, as soon as Swim falls asweep."

Hmmm, that was interesting. It appeared that the little snipe had some ideas of his own.

Well, we dogs weren't invited to lunch, which

was okay. I mean, we had other things to do and if Slim thought he was too good to share his meal with two loyal, hardworking ranch dogs, that was just fine. I wasn't too fond of Vienna sausage anyway, although if he had . . . but he didn't.

Well, it was definitely a hot, still summer day, and I was carrying around this heavy coat of hair, and all at once the timing seemed perfect for a nice roll in Emerald Pond.

Emerald Pond, you might recall, was my own private bath and spa. It lay about halfway between the house and the corrals, shaded by large elm trees and fed by mineral springs whose life-enhancing trickle could be traced to the overflow of the septic tank.

Many a time I had dragged myself to the edge of Emerald Pond, wondering if I could summon the energy to wade out into those healing waters—and we're talking about tired and exhausted, sometimes even injured, burdened down by all the responsibilities of running a ranch with very little help or cooperation from anyone else, solving one mystery after another, working day and night and yet somehow finding the time and energy to bark at the mail truck every morning at ten o'clock.

Really messed up, in other words, but five minutes of rolling in those fragrant waters had never failed to snatch me back from the edge of the brink and restore my spirits.

And it was into those very waters that I now plunged. I waded out brisket-deep and collapsed, rolled around, kicked my legs in the air, and indulged myself in the kind of joyous barking that comes to a cowdog at such moments.

That done, I scampered out onto dry land,

gave myself a good shake, rolled in the grass, and leaped to my feet—a new dog. In the meantime, Drover had ventured over to the pond's edge and had tapped one paw into the water.

I just couldn't understand . . . I was on the point of giving the little mutt a lecture on Health Care and Beauty Aids when my ears picked up a sound in the distance.

I froze and listened. "What was that?"

"Well, I think it was the sewer."

"No, no, a sound, an unusual sound." I lifted my ears and listened. There it was again. "Drover, unless I miss my guess, someone has just come out of the house and slammed the screen door."

"And that means they didn't come out the window."

"Exactly. Now the only question remaining is, who could it be?"

"Yeah, and that depends on who came out the door."

"Exactly. And we're about to find out. Come on, Drover, to the yard gate, on the double!"

And with that, we went streaking away from the banks of Emerald Pond and made a lightning dash to the house.

Little did I know or suspect that within the hour, I would be forced to eat strawberry ice cream. And even littler did I suspect that I would be given a ride in a spaceship.

You probably don't believe that, but just wait and see.

CHAPTER FOUR

Running Scientific Tests on Strawberry Ice Cream

It was Little Alfred who had just come out of the house. He was standing on the sidewalk in his jeans and T-shirt and boots, and he was calling our names:

"Here, Hankie! Here, Dwovoo!"

You know, there's something special about a little boy calling his dogs. And it's especially special if you happen to be a dog, as I happen to be. It makes a guy feel . . .

As I went trotting up to the yard gate, I was shocked to see that Little Alfred's mouth was covered with BLOOD! Okay, some unspeakable villain had punched my little pal in the mouth and perhaps even knocked out several of his teeth, and anybody who'd punch a little kid around deserved just what he was fixing to get, and what he was fixing to get was the Head of . . .

On the other hand, he wasn't crying, which was a little puzzling. You'd think a boy who'd just been slugged in the mouth by a bully would have . . .

I went streaking through the yard gate, vaguely aware that the yard was Forbidden Territory but more than vaguely aware that Sally May had left the ranch. In other words, what she didn't know she would never find out.

But even more important, if she had known that I was rushing into Forbidden Territory to defend her little boy against the attack of some heartless bully, she would have been the first to put a thorn in my crown.

I rushed to his side. I barked and wagged my tail, waiting for him to reveal the location of the brute. On the other hand, why was he laughing? And why did he pinch the end of my nose?

Well, the least I could do, it seemed to me, was to clean up his face a little bit, and so I . . . ketchup?

Okay, it appeared that we'd gotten ourselves all stirred up over . . . Drover had jumped to hasty . . . sometimes we get faulty readings on our instruments, don't you know, and . . .

The boy had been eating ketchup, see, and a fair percentage of it had ended up on his face, is all. No blood, no violence, no bully to take care of. I'd sort of suspected ketchup from the very beginning, but a guy can't really follow his hunch until he runs a more detailed analysis.

Don't you see.

Well, that was a nice turn of events and I went ahead and cleaned him up, knowing that his mother would have done the same thing if she'd been around. Ketchup is pretty good stuff, and this little task turned out to be more pleasant than I had expected.

Yes, I just kept cleaning and cleaning until the boy pushed me away and said, "Quit wicking me on the mouff, Hankie!" At that point, I stopped wicking him on the mouff, so to speak, and returned all four paws to the ground.

Sally May would have been proud. The boy's face was spotless.

It was then that he opened the screen door and called us over. And with a twinkle in his eyes, he said, "Come on, doggies, wet's go in the house!"

I looked at Drover and he looked at me. "Did you hear what he said, Drover?"

"Who?"

"Whom do you think?"

"Well, I don't know. Little Alfred?"

"Very good. Did you hear what he said?"

"I think he said the house is wet."

"No. You garbled the translation. He said, 'Wet's go in the house.' In kid language, 'wet' means 'let.'"

"I'll be derned. What would he say if the house got wet?"

"He would say, 'The house is moist.'"

"I'll be derned. Do you reckon a pipe broke?"

"What?"

"I said, how'd all that water get in the house?"

I looked deeply into his eyes and wondered what kind of terrible injury had caused such a mess. "Drover, you've missed the whole point of this conversation. Little Alfred has invited us into the house."

"Not me. I think I'll pass."

"Sally May is gone for the day and she'll never suspect a thing."

"Yeah, but you know about me and water. Just give me the good old dry land, that's the place for me."

I heaved a sigh and shook my head in despair. "Fine, Drover. You stay out here and snap at the flies. I'll accept Alfred's invitation and go inside. You'll be sorry, of course, but you can't help it that you're a total moron."

I turned my thoughts away from the depressing task of carrying on a normal conversation with Drover. Little Alfred was holding open the screen door and pointing the way inside. I didn't know to what I owed this honor, but it seemed only decent to accept it.

I went through the door and sat down in the utility room. Little Alfred closed the screen, being careful not to let it slam. Oh yes, Slim must have been taking a nap and the boy didn't want to disturb him.

That impressed me. A lot of these kids would just go slam-banging through the house and never give a thought to anybody else. Alfred had his flies . . . flaws, that is, but you could tell that his momma had tried to teach him some manners.

He gave me a wink and a smile and went tiptoeing into the kitchen. Exactly what the wink and smile meant, and why he chose to travel on tiptoes, I didn't know. But I soon found out.

He sneaky-walked through the kitchen and pushed a chair up to the refriginator . . . frigeriginator . . . the icebox door. He opened the top door (there were two: a big one on bottom and a smaller one above it).

Very strange. Fog rolled out of the top compartment. Several clouds of fog. My goodness, the

34

weather must have been changing or something.

He stuck his hand and arm into the foggy compartment and came out with . . . well, with a great big grin on his face, for one thing, but what was that carton in his hand? A round carton.

He left the door open and the fog continued to roll out. He climbed down from the chair and fetched a spoon out of one of the kitchen drawers. Then he sat down in the middle of the floor and told me to sit down beside him.

Okay, I could handle that. I sat down beside him and watched as he pried the lid off the top of the mysterious carton. The lid hit the floor and rolled around. I stared at the contents of the alleged carton.

It was pink. It was hard. It smelled like something a dog might want to, well, eat, so to speak. I scootched a bit closer and watched this procedure with a, uh, higher level of interest.

I mean, I take a special interest in these kids and their activities, whether they're involved in church, school, 4-H, or . . . well, food. Food is a very important component in the development of a child, and it sure did smell good.

Kind of sweet, almost like strawberries and cream.

I watched as Little Alfred took the spoon in his

fist and dug into the . . . whatever it was. I watched,
with all the concern of a parent or guardian, as he
moved the spoon to his mouth.

I moved my paws up and down and whined.
I whapped my tail several times on the floor. I
scootched even closer. Like any parent or guardian,
I wanted to know what the boy was eating. I
mean, these kids will put any kind of garbage into
their mouths, and a guy sure wants to know . . .

"Want some ice cweam, Hankie?"

Oh-h-h-h-h-h-h, so that was it! Ice cream, huh? By George, it had been a long time since I'd tested any ice cream, and yes, I felt it was my duty to, uh, check it out.

He scooped out a big hunk and I gobbled it down. Strawberry ice cream, and pretty derned good. On the other hand, I'd never been one to leap to any scientific conclusions based on a single test, and I felt a certain craving . . . need, that is, to submit the ice cream to more rigorous testing procedures.

Hence, when he offered me a second bite, I did what had to be done—took it, chewed it up, and swallowed it down.

Boy, was that stuff good! But on the other hand, this was Sally May's child and I sure didn't want to take any chances . . . some kids are allergic to ice cream, see, makes 'em break out in hives and stuff, and they tell me that strawberry is the world's worst about causing hives.

One more test run, just to be sure. I mean, if the boy had broken out in hives, I never would have forgiven myself. I took one last bite.

Then he took a bite, and then he took another bite and that didn't seem fair, him taking two bites to my one, and I whined and thumped my tail until he came across with one last big scoop of, uh, test material.

Boy, was that stuff...headache? That stuff was delicious but for some reason it was giving me a headache. I pawed the spot above my eyes where the pain was centered, and after a bit it went away.

Hey, our tests had turned up a possibly dangerous side effect—it caused headaches! Well, you know me, when duty calls, I get with the program. This stuff needed to be tested and tested and TESTED, never mind the cost or sacrifice, and before I knew it, me and Little Alfred had tested the whole entire carton.

CHAPTER FIVE

The Spaceship
Episode

Well, I ended up getting three headaches out of the testing deal, but that was a small price to pay for all the peace of mind it brought.

Alfred looked into the empty carton and grinned. "The ice cweam's all gone, Hankie."

I burped . . . belched, that is, and listened to a certain creaking noise in my stomach. You'd have thought that I'd just eaten a squeaky gate or something, the way it sounded. And I did notice a certain fullness about my midsection, felt like I'd just swallowed an inner tube. And a squeaky gate.

And half a sack of dog food.

And three bales of hay.

Boy, I was one full dog! Alfred crossed the

kitchen and went out into the utility room. Naturally, I followed. Had a little trouble walking, to tell you the truth, but I'm no quitter. I forced my legs to carry the load and they did the job, but I was kind of glad I didn't have to walk very far.

I supposed that we were going back outside, but he stopped in front of his ma's washer and dryer. "Hankie," he whispered, "you want to go for a wide in a weal spaceship?"

Ride in a spaceship? Well . . . not really. Ordinarily I thrive on adventure, but I had just done quite a bit of thriving on strawberry ice cream and . . .

Spaceship, huh? I hadn't realized that Sally May owned one. I ran my eyes around and across the utility room and didn't see anything that resembled a spaceship. On the other hand, there might have been a few things I didn't know about spaceships, such as what one might look like.

But as far as me making a trip into space right then . . . well, I had quite a bit of work lined up for the afternoon, and the thought had occurred to me that a nap might fit in there somewhere. I mean, all that lab work and testing and stuff had left me feeling kind of full and drowsy.

And, come to think about it, I wasn't exactly

sure where SPACE was or how long it would take to go there. I had never been to space.

Maybe we could ride the spaceship another time.

Alfred opened the door . . . hatch . . . whatever, of the clothes dryer and pointed inside. "Hankie, this is my X-Wing Fighter. It's a weal spaceship, and it can fwy off to the stars!"

No kidding? I peered inside. It looked pretty muchly like a clothes dryer to me, but again, I was no expert on space stuff. I had my hands full trying to run a ranch on Planet Earth.

The boy grabbed me around the chest and lifted me off the ground and tried to poke me into the cabin of the X-Wing Fighter. I, uh, resisted this opportunity.

I mean, let's face it. This kid had been known to pull pranks, and more than once I had been the victim. On the whole, little Alfred was a good boy, but he did have an ornery streak and my trust of his motives did have its limits.

In other words, I wasn't interested in being sent off alone into space in his X-Wing Fighter. Now, if he'd offered to go along and drive the thing, well, that might have been different, but as far as me flying off into space by myself . . . no.

I guess he figgered that out, because after trying several times to poke my back legs into the cockpit, he gave up and set me back on the floor.

He pressed his lips together and frowned at me. "Hankie, what's wong wiff you? Don't you want to wide in my spaceship?"

I thumped my tail on the floor and, well, belched again (sure was full of strawberry ice cream), and avoided the focus of his eyes. I hated to disappoint the kid, but this just wasn't the time for . . .

"Okay, Hankie, I'll get in first. Then you can join me."

Well . . . maybe and maybe not. We'd just have to take this deal one step at a time, but his offering to go in first was definitely the first step.

Sure enough, he climbed into the cockpit and settled himself into the . . . well, there really wasn't a seat in the thing, just a round something-or-other made of metal, looked kind of uncomfortable to me, but he settled into it and didn't seem to mind.

Then he took the . . . I guess it was a steering wheel, although I couldn't really see it very well . . . he took the steering wheel in both hands, and I'll be derned if that spaceship didn't make a roaring sound—you know, motors or jets engines, rockets, whatever you call those things.

At first I thought Alfred was making the sound. He's pretty good at making loud noises, you know, but then I wasn't so sure. By George, it sounded pretty real to me, so maybe that thing WAS an X-Wing Fighter after all.

I couldn't imagine why Sally May had bought a spaceship and installed it in her utility room, but you never know. Maybe it was one of those new models that served as a spaceship part of the time and as a clothes dryer part of the time.

The boy did a fifteen-second burn on his engines and then shut them off. "Come on, Hankie, get in and wet's go for a wide."

Well . . . why not? I coiled my legs under me and hopped up into the cockpit and took my place in the copilot's seat. Alfred took the controls again, fired his engines, and away we went at a high rate of speed.

After a bit, Captain Alfred came on the radio. "Captain Alfood to Hankie, appwoaching Pwanet Venus!" I gazed out the pothole . . . porthole, I guess it was, gazed out the porthole and sure enough, there was Planet Venus passing before our very eyes.

"Captain Alfood to Hankie, appwoaching Pwanet Okwahoma!" By George, there it was, Planet Oklahoma in all its splinter. "Captain Alfood to

Hankie, I'm fixing to weave the ship and make a space walk. You dwive now."

Roger, Captain!

I took over command of the ship, did a quick scan of the instrument panel just to be sure that all systems were up and functioning. Everything checked out.

While I was absorbed in the instrument check and making double-sure that we didn't fly too close to Planet Oklahoma, Captain Alfred slipped into his space suit and began his spacewalk maneuver. He exited the ship through the pothole and . . .

Slammed the hatch? All at once it was pretty dark in there. Captain Alfred grinned at me through the pothole window and waved. Then I seemed to hear him climbing on top of the ship. Maybe he was checking for leaks or something, or maybe . . .

HUH?

Fellers, something was happening to the ship!

MAYDAY, MAYDAY!!

RED ALERT!

CODE THREE!

DEFCON FIVE!

YIKES!

All at once I lost control of the ship. My controls

went dead, my instruments blanked out, the ship went into a deadly spiral dive, and holy smokes, I was tumbling around and around and around.

And around and around, and bumping my head!

The cabin temperature was rising and I caught the scent of heated metal. We had a fire in the cockpit! We were falling out of control! I was tumbling and flying around and getting beat to smithereens!

I don't know how I did it, but at the very last moment I pulled her out of that deadly spiral dive and executed a smooth landing. Next thing I knew, Little Alfred had opened the hatch and was pulling me out of the burning cockpit.

Just in time too. I mean, the smoke and flames had just about gotten me.

He pulled me out of the burning wreckage, boy, what a crash, and let me tell you, he looked scared. I could understand that. It had been pretty tough for both of us, but even tougher for him than for me. At least I'd been inside the cockpit. That poor kid had been up on top of the ship!

We were just lucky we didn't lose him.

At that point, he said something that I didn't understand. He said, "Sowwy, Hankie. I wondered what that button would do."

Button? Didn't make any sense to me. The kid must have been scared out of his wits, didn't know what he was saying.

Well, you can't believe how glad I was to plant my paws back on good old Planet Earth! It would be a long time before I ever climbed into another one of those spaceships.

I checked my body for damage: no busted bones, no blood, no serious cuts, just a lot of bruises that didn't show. In other words, I had somehow managed to walk away...

But I did feel dizzy and noticed a certain queasy feeling in my stomach. All that tumbling around. And around and around, and walking straight seemed out of the question as I staggered across the floor, feeling dizzy and more than slightly queasy in the stomach.

And all at once I thought of strawberry ice cream and wished I hadn't. If a guy knew for sure that he was going to crash a spaceship, the last thing in the world he'd want to eat would be strawberry...

You know, I was feeling kind of sick. Course, even your most experienced pilots get a touch of... boy, was I feeling lousy! And dizzy. Ran into the trash can and bounced off the kitchen cabinet, and just the thought of strawberry ice cream made me want to...

Uh-oh.

In spite of injuries and dizziness, I managed to stagger through the kitchen and into the living room. I needed to go outside, is what I really needed, but the door... and there wasn't time anyway, so I...

I, uh, found this nice little spot behind Sally May's couch. It was quiet, isolated, dark. I guessed that nobody had ever visited that deserted piece of carpet, and probably nobody ever would. Hence, nobody would ever know . . .

I felt much better now. Most of the dizziness and so forth had vanished, and I made my way around the front of the couch and headed for the back door.

But as I passed the front of the couch, a long bony hand *reached out and grabbed me,* and a mysterious voice said, "What are you doing in here, pooch?!"

CHAPTER SIX

Attacked by
the Couch Monster

Have you ever run into a Couch Monster? Neither had I. They aren't too common in our country, but it certainly appeared that I had just been grabbed by one.

I'm not sure what causes a couch to turn into a Couch Monster, but I can report what I learned about this one. When I entered that living room, the couch was just a couch. But as I was leaving, it suddenly sprouted an arm that reached out and grabbed me, and acquired a voice, a terrible voice, that rumbled, "WHAT ARE YOU DOING IN HERE, POOCH?!"

Scared the living daylights out of me. Maybe my guilt feelings about being in Sally May's living room had something to do with how badly it scared me, because I was indeed feeling a few pricks of guilt and remorse about, well, being in the house and so forth.

And I sure wasn't expecting to be assaulted by a Couch Monster in a semidarkened living room in the middle of the day. A guy hears about those things happening to other dogs, but he tends to think, "Nah, it'll never happen to me."

But it sure as heck did happen to me. When that hand reached out and grabbed me by the scruff of the neck, I let out a squeak, lifted the hair on my back, and went to Full Stampede to the left.

It was then that I saw the Ghostly Form rising from the couch. Yes sir, this ghost or evil spirit, call it what you wish, this THING in human form rose out of the cushions of the couch and sat up. It had a long nose, a beard, and hair down in its eyes.

I bristled up like a cornered coyote, bared my fangs, and barked as I'd never barked before.

That should have done the trick, but to my astonishment the THING continued to rise until it left the couch from which it had come like a wisp of smoke rising from a fire.

It planted its feet upon the floor, reared up to its full height, made claws with its hands, and twisted its eyes and mouth into a horrible mask.

And then, claws extended into a grabbing-and-killing position, it began lurching toward me—uttering a terrible growl that froze my blood in its vaynes.

Vanes.

Vaines.

Vessels.

Froze my blood in its vessels.

You think I didn't bark at that thing? I not only gave it the whole book on barking, but I also retreated a few steps to the northwest, just in case it . . .

And it did! IT CAME AFTER ME! Hey, that was all I needed to know about Couch Monsters: They ate dogs. And with that, I said good-bye to barking and went ripping out of the living room and into the kitchen, did a little slipping and sliding on that slick linoleum floor, and vanished into a closet in the back bedroom.

It was there in the darkness of the closet that I heard a thunder of laughter, and then a familiar voice: "What's wrong, Hankie, did ya think I was going to eat ya?"

Okay, what we had here . . . once again Slim had . . . have we discussed stupid childish cowboy pranks? He had pulled that stupid childish monster trick on me so many times, you'd think I would have . . . you'd think a grown man could find something better to do with his time.

But the bottom line is that a dog can't afford to take chances. Once in a great while he'll come out on the short end of the . . . let's just drop it.

I crept out of the closet and peered around the corner and into the kitchen. I wagged my tail. Sure enough, there was Slim, pulling on his boots. When he saw me, he chuckled to himself and said, "Look at the hair on that dog's back!"

I barked at him one last time, just to let him know what I thought of his twisted sense of humor.

"Now, now, Hankie, don't be bitter. We was only having a little fun." Little Alfred appeared at that moment, whistling a tune and looking up at the ceiling. Slim forked him with his eyes. "Say, Hotrod, who let that dog in the house?"

"Oh, he just swipped in, I guess."

"Uh-huh. And if your momma was to walk in right now, I might be a-wearin' her iron skillet around my neck. Let's try to keep the livestock outside, hear?"

"Okay, Swim. It was an accident."

"Yalp."

That was odd. All signs and symptoms of the Ice Cream Experiment had disappeared—the carton and the lid—and somebody had even shut the freezer door. Slim would never know the full extent of what he had missed.

He finished pulling on his boots and stood up. "Well, we'd better saddle me a bronc and see if we can put that old hookin' bull back where he belongs."

He started toward the back door but then stopped and sniffed the air. "Boy, I need to warsh my socks. Smells like a sewer in here."

Funny, I hadn't noticed the smell of his socks, but then I'd had my mind on other things.

We went trooping out of the house, picked up Mister Look-at-the-Clouds at the yard gate, hooked the stock trailer onto Slim's pickup, and pulled down to the corrals.

Slim had kept up a young bay horse the night before. He caught him and led him into the saddle lot and threw a saddle on him. While he tightened the cinches, he talked out loud to himself.

"If I have to rope that old bull, I might wish I'd taken a better horse. I've never roped anything big on this owl-headed thang, and there's not much tellin' what he might do." He stopped and thought a moment. "In fact, I believe I'll just . . . nah, it's too hot to gather the horse pasture. We'll do what needs to be done, won't we, Button?"

Little Alfred smiled. "I'll wope that bull, if you'll wet me."

Slim led the horse out the gate and latched it behind him. "I wish I could, son, 'cause roping bulls is sometimes hard on clothes and old men."

"I woped me a chicken today."

"I'll bet you did. When it comes to slinging that twine, you're a regular holy terrier."

Slim loaded his horse into the trailer. Little Alfred watched. "I wike to wope, and I'm pwetty good."

"That's fine, Button, just keep a-throwin' and keep a-learnin'. One of these days you'll be as good with a rope as I am, and probably just as rich."

"Are you wich, Swim?"

Slim hitched up his jeans and smiled. "Well now, I'm rich in the things that matter to me. I'm proud of who I am and what I do. To me, that's rich. There's a song that says just what I'm a-tryin' to tell you, Button. Let's see if I can remember how it goes."

I didn't know old Slim could even carry a tune, but by George he did. Here's how it went.

Just Another Cowboy Day

This morning at five I got out of bed,
Boiled some coffee and toasted some bread.
I pulled on the jeans I'd left throwed on
    the chair,

55

And brushed all the roostertails out of
   my hair.

My eyes was all soggy, I couldn't see squat.
I tripped on the dog on my way to the pot.
I said to myself as I kicked him away,
"It's another cowboy day."

   It's another cowboy day
   Diggin' them postholes and pitchin'
      that hay.
   It's another cowboy day,
   Just another cowboy day.

I went to the mirror and stood there a while.
The face starin' back at me looked pretty wild.
If eyes was like teeth, I could take out the red
And soak 'em in Polident next to my bed.

Old Arthur was hurtin', my shoulder was sore.
Sometimes I think I can't take any more.
I've left many times but always I stayed
For another cowboy day.

   It's another cowboy day
   Diggin' them postholes and pitchin'
      that hay.

It's another cowboy day,
Just another cowboy day.

I went to the barn and fed my old horse,
Me and that rascal have been through
    the course.
He ain't all that good but he ain't all that bad.
Old Dunny's the best friend that I've ever
    I had.

Old Dunny and me, we cut through the
    breeze
As morning was paintin' the tops of the trees.
"Oh Lord, give me more," that's all I could say,
"Just another cowboy day."

It's another cowboy day
Diggin' them postholes and pitchin'
    that hay.
It's another cowboy day,
Just another cowboy day.

By the time Slim finished the song, Little
Alfred was playing bulldozer in the dirt with a
piece of wood. "Well Button, does that make any
sense to you?"

"Nope, but it's a pwetty song."

Slim smiled. "Sometimes it don't make much sense to me either. Well, load up. We've got things to do and places to go."

"Can I wide in the back wiff my doggies?"

Slim frowned. "Why don't you ride up front with me? Your ma would feel better if you did. And you never can tell, I might need some help drivin'."

"Can Hankie and Dwover wide up fwont too?"

"Now Button, we don't need to be spoilin' them dogs. Next thing you know, they'll think they've got a constitutional right..."

"Pweeze, Swim, just this once."

Slim shook his head and moved his lips. "Oh, all right, but just this once."

"Yippee! Come on, doggies, we get to wide in the fwont!"

The three of us made a dash for the pickup, while Slim came along behind, talking to himself.

"I know better than to start this foolishness. Once you spoil a ranch dog, he ain't worth shootin' from then on. Course, them two dogs was born worthless, but we ain't going to make a habit of this ridin' in front, you hear what I'm sayin'? Just this once."

"Okay, Swim."

Slim opened the door and the three of us

climbed up on the seat. At the mailbox, Slim stopped and looked both ways before he pulled onto the caliche road.

He wrinkled up his nose. "Boy, this pickup sure stinks. If that's my socks again, I'm going to burn them thangs."

We turned onto the road and off we went to the pasture. If I had known what was waiting for us up there, I might had chosen to stay at home.

CHAPTER SEVEN

We Meet the Horrible Hairy Hooking Bull

There were two roads that led up to the north pasture. One went straight north through the middle pasture, and the other looped around to the west.

The one that looped around to the west and followed the canyon pasture fence was the longer of the two, which naturally meant that the other was the shorter of the two, right? It was shorter but you had to open two gates to get to the north pasture.

Slim took the long route so's he could get by without having to stop, get out, open the gate, get back in, drive through, get out again, shut the gate, get back in, and drive on. You see, Little Alfred wasn't quite big and stout enough to open and shut pasture gates, and while Slim was old enough and stout enough, he had a small lazy streak and a weakness for using cattle guards instead of gates.

So we took the long route up to the north pasture. As you will soon see, this will become a crucial piece of information in the unfolding drama of The Hooking Bull. If Little Alfred had been faced with two pasture gates to open . . . well, you'll find out soon enough.

As soon as we turned off the main road, Little Alfred started pestering Slim to let him drive the pickup. Slim growled and grumbled about the hazards of doing such things, but since he'd been the one who'd brought the subject up in the first place, he didn't have much chance of winning that argument.

So the boy crawled over in his lap and took the steering wheel in both hands. I'll admit this made me nervous. It reminded me of the time I'd gone on a spaceship ride with the little stinkpot. I won't say that his driving had caused that crash, but I won't say that it didn't either.

But this time he did all right, kept the pickup mostly in the tracks without too much wandering around in the pasture. After he'd steered a while, with Slim running the gas and the brake, he decided he needed to handle that department too, so Slim gave him a tryout, running the gas and brakes.

First time he hit the brake pedal, me and Drover got ourselves introduced to the dashboard. After that, he didn't punch it so hard, but we dogs took no chances. We were braced and welded against the back of that seat.

Slim let him drive all the way up to the cattle guard that led into the north pasture and then he took the controls back, saying, "Button, that cattle guard's about as wide as it needs to be, and I'll take 'er from here."

When we crossed the cattle guard, Slim scanned the horizon and started talking to himself. "Now let's get organized here. This time of day in the summer, them cattle are most likely to be at the windmill. We'll check there first for that bull."

He threw the gearshift up into Grandma Low and we started down a washed-out trail that led into a ravine. When we reached the bottom, we saw the windmill up ahead. Sure enough, fifty or sixty cows and calves were lazing around the water tank.

"There he is," said Slim in a low voice, "and look

at the size of that feller! That, boys, is a lot of bull."

I followed the direction of his gaze and ... hmm, yes, that was a big bull, all right, with a nasty hump in his back and a wide head like a catfish and a mean-looking set of horns.

Drover was staring at the clouds and hadn't seen the bull yet.

"You know, Drover, if Slim needs any help on this assignment, it might be a good time to let you get some experience."

"Really?"

"There's no substitute for experience, son, and I know that I have a tendency to hog all the excitement. Yes, by George, we'll just let you solo on this one."

"Gosh, thanks, Hank. Are you sure I can handle it?"

"Uh, well, that's the whole idea behind hands-on training, Drover, finding answers to those little questions. And yes, I'm confident that you will learn a great deal from this experience."

"Oh boy, I can hardly wait. Just bark at him?"

"Oh yeah, bark at him and maybe bite him on the nose if he tries to attack."

His eyes went blank. "Attack? What kind of cow is this?"

"Well, it's not exactly a cow, Drover, more of a bull than a cow."

"A bull?"

"That's correct, just an ordinary garden variety of bull who happens to be in the wrong pasture and has forgotten how to get back home. Nothing special, in other words."

All at once the runt stopped looking at the clouds and squinted his eyes at the cattle in front of us. I heard him gulp.

"That wouldn't be him right over there, would

it? With the hump in his back and the big horns?"

"Don't worry about the hump, son. Camels have two humps and they're the friendliest animals you ever saw. The hump means nothing, almost nothing at all."

"Yeah, but look at those horns!"

"Once again, the horns mean almost nothing. The idea is to stay out of the way of the horns. I noticed that his eyes had crossed. "Drover, something's wrong with your eyes."

"No, it's my leg. It's killing me."

"What I'm looking at is not your leg, unless you've moved it up around your nose."

"No, it hurts to move it. Just the least little movement brings on this terrible pain. Maybe I'd better sit this one out, Hank."

"Forget that, son. You're fixing to make a solo run."

"Oh, my leg!"

By this time Slim had unloaded his horse and led him up to the pickup. He pulled all his cinches down tight.

"Button, I'm going to try to drive that bull back where he belongs. If he'll drive, I'll take him up that hill and through that gate yonder, and I'll be back in ten minutes. While I'm gone, I want you to stay in the pickup, you hear?"

The boy nodded.

"'Cause if you get out and go to foolin' around with these baby calves, some of those mommas are liable to think you're a prowlin' coyote instead of Sally May's darlin' child, and one of 'em might try to get into your pocket."

The boy nodded.

"Now," Slim pressed his lips together, "if the bull don't want to cooperate, I may have to take more drastic measures, such as put my nylon around his horns and drag him into the trailer. It could get a little western, so keep out of the way."

"Okay, Swim. But I don't want you to wope the bull."

"Neither do I, Button, but that's up to him. I'll take Hank with me."

HUH?

I, uh, eased down on the floorboard and tried to make myself invisible. Maybe if I flattened myself on the floor, he might think . . .

"Hank, come on. I may need you to put some bite on that bull's nose."

At that moment, Drover spoke. "I think Slim wants you for something."

"No, I think he was calling you."

"No, he said 'Hank,' I'm almost sure he did, and my name's Drover, so I guess he decided to put in the first string, and I'll just have to sit this one out."

"I'll bet that breaks your heart."

"Yeah, I was sure looking forward to going a round or two with that old bull."

"Hank! Get out of that pickup, let's go."

I pushed myself up and, hmm, noticed that my legs were trembling. "All right, you little weasel, I'll do your dirty work for you, but this will go in my report—every word of it."

"Oh rats, but I'll bark from here, Hank. Maybe that'll help."

"Thanks a lot, Drover."

"Oh, it was the least I could do."

"Yes, I'm aware of that, you little . . ."

It seems that Slim got impatient and reached in and grabbed me by the tail and hauled me outside, and that really wasn't necessary, I'd only wanted to take care of a little business with Drover and . . .

Slim stepped into the saddle and pulled his hat down. Then he glanced down at me. "You ready for this, pooch? Let's go exercise that old bull."

He rode forward through the herd. The cattle stared at him with big stupid eyes and parted to let him through. I fell in behind the horse. My enthusiasm for this project was, well, running at a fairly low level, mainly because my involvement was depriving Drover of valuable, much needed experience.

Slim maneuvered his horse around until only one animal stood in his path. The bull's ears were cocked and he was watching the horse's every move.

"Hyah, go on, bull! Get on out of here!"

The bull sensed that he had been cut off from the herd. He moved to the right and Slim cut him off. He moved to the left and Slim turned him back again. The bull shook his head and stood his ground.

Slim took down his catch rope, pulled the loop down to where it was just a knot, and let out about seven feet of slack. Then he flipped the rope so that the knot popped Mr. Bull on the nose.

WHAP!

That got his attention! He whirled around and started trotting away from the herd. Well, that had been easy enough, and I figgered this might be a good time for me to install my Anti-Bull Procedures. Barking at the top of my lungs, I rushed past the horse and sank my teeth into the left rear hock of this large but cowardly . . .

One detail a guy tends to forget about these bulls is that, while they're very large and appear to be slow and dim-witted, they're actually none of those things except large. I mean, it's hard to believe that a bull weighing in at 1,300 or 1,400 pounds can turn on a dime and give you the change.

But they can. And he did.

And I sure wasn't expecting him to do that. And I don't think I'll tell you what happened next.

What Happened Next

Hey, I had worked bulls before. I knew they were capable of inflicting big damage if they got half a chance, but I also knew that once you get a bull turned and running off in the right direction, 97.4 percent of the time he'll keep going and won't turn to fight.

So I played the percentages, right? When the numbers are on your side, everything's supposed to turn out just fine, and what more can a dog do?

Okay, I'll tell you what happened after I bit that stupid bull on the heels, but I'm not proud of it and there's no reason for blabbing it all over the country.

I sank my teeth into his left hock, little suspecting that he might kick me into a low polar orbit with the right one, and never dreaming that he could do it in the blink of an eye. But he derned sure did.

Kicked me dead-center in the rib cage, and I thought I had been run over by a large truck. All at once I saw red checkers and skyrockets exploding behind my eyes. I couldn't breathe. I couldn't think. I couldn't move.

I don't know how far I flew through the air, but it wasn't far enough. I landed nose-first in the side of a sandhill. I lay there on the ground, gasping for breath and trying to restart my heart, when I began to realize that this killer hooking bull wasn't finished with me.

It wasn't enough that he'd broken the Law of Averages and taken a really cheap shot and kicked the absolute stuffing out of me. No, he wanted some more, and HERE HE CAME!

Any bull that would beat up on a handicapped dog is beneath contempt, but he loaded me up on his horns and pitched me into the Ozone Layer of the atmosphere.

I landed in an awkward heap in the middle of a sagebrush, and I remember with perfect clarity the thought that came to my mind when I hit: "Enough of this nonsense, let's go to the house!"

But the drama was just beginning, as it turned

out. Slim popped the bull again and tried to turn him back to the northeast, but Mr. Bull seemed to be enjoying this, and instead of running away, he dropped his head and charged Slim's horse.

They got out of the way just in time. Slim rode a short distance away and started building a loop in his rope. His eyes had settled into a tight squint and the muscles in his jaws were working.

"You all right, Hankie?"

Arg, gasp, urg, wheeze, no, not really.

"Get up and let's teach this old general who's boss around here."

Um, no thanks. I already knew who was boss.

Slim shook out his loop and held it shoulder-high. He moved his horse toward the bull and tried to coax him into running. And I knew why he tried to do that. You see, it's much easier to rope an animal that's running away from you than to rope one that's facing you.

I knew that, even though I myself don't rope. I had watched Slim and Loper in action before, and I seem to have an amazing memory for such details. It's just part of being a cowdog.

But the bull didn't go for it. He was on the fight and he had no intention of running anywhere. He perked his ears, bellered, pawed the ground, and dared Slim to make the next move.

And Slim did. Instead of throwing your standard head-or-horn loop, as he would have done if the bull had run away, he turned his horse to the left and flicked out a hoolihan.

That hoolihan is a slick loop. It's quick, like a cobra striking its victim. No twirl, no warning, just swish and jerk slack. Slim's a pretty good hand with the hoolihan, and he nailed his loop to Mr. Bull's horns.

It was a great throw and one of the biggest mistakes he'd made all week.

He popped his slack, turned his horse, gave

him the spurs, and headed for the stock trailer without even looking back. He should have looked back, because at that very moment Mr. Bull turned and ran in the opposite direction.

I saw what was coming and I tried to bark a warning, but it was already too late. The dye had already been cast into the washtub. Also, I couldn't even breathe, let alone bark.

To appreciate what happened next, you must remember: 1) the home-end of Slim's rope was tied solid to the saddle horn; 2) he was riding a young horse that probably had never been married to a full-grown bull; 3) horse and bull were running hard in opposite directions; and 4) nylon ropes don't break.

When they hit the ends of that rope at the same time, the wreck began. It jerked Slim's horse completely off his feet and he landed on top of Slim. I mean, all I could see of that cowboy was two hands, one boot, and part of a dirty felt hat, sticking out from under a horse that was wallowing around and trying to get up.

I had witnessed a few wrecks in my time, but this one looked about as nasty as any I could imagine. And it wasn't over yet.

The jerk whipped the bull around so hard that he swapped ends and came out of it facing Slim and the horse. And instead of teaching him a lesson, it had just made him madder than ever.

That bull's head was shaking with rage. I heard him snort. I heard Little Alfred scream. I heard Slim let out a groan from underneath the horse.

And then, before my very eyes, the bull lowered his head and charged the horse! And holy smokes, all at once we had a terrorized colt on top of a smashed cowboy, being charged by a huge horned hooking bull that was mad enough to finish the job he'd just started.

And don't forget that rope. The horse and the bull were still tied together by that rope.

And don't forget that the Head of Ranch Security had been wounded in action and was in no position to rush to anybody's defense. I mean, I was still trying to get my first breath. I was crippled and badly damaged and beaten to a pulp.

The bull waded into the wreckage and started working that poor colt over with his horns—and if you think the colt was "poor," just think about what was underneath him: Slim.

Wham! Wham! Thud! Snort!

Oh, that bull had no mercy! Good grief, hadn't he done enough damage? Did he have to keep on beating on that poor colt with his horns?

By George, when I saw that, I started getting

mad. I jacked myself up off the ground and yelled, "Drover, are you going to stand there and watch this outrage? What are you waiting for? Get your skinny, worthless little stub tail out here and draw some blood!"

"Well . . . you go first, Hank, and then I'll come."

"I can't go first, you moron! I'm wounded and damaged beyond repair. We've got a cowboy on the ground and he needs help right now, and you're next in the chain of command. Attack, charge, Red Alert!"

"Oh my gosh! Well, I guess I can . . . I sure hope this old leg of mine . . ."

I'll give him credit for trying. He jumped out of the pickup and ran straight for the bull, yipping and squeaking. I'm sure the bull got a chuckle out of that—a sawed-off, stub-tailed squeakbox coming out on the field of battle to do something or other.

When Drover was about two feet away, the bull made a run at him. Drover not only changed directions in the blink of an eye, but he also destroyed half the sagebrush in that pasture, getting back to the pickup.

The bull watched this with his wicked, heartless eyes, and it even appeared to me that he was smirking. Then he turned back to his main source of entertainment, beating up on the colt.

By this time, the colt had wallowed to his feet. He was moon-eyed and trembling all over, waiting to see what this dragon of a bull would try to do to him next.

My eyes darted to Slim. He was lying facedown in the sand. He hadn't moved. I could see that he needed my help. I took a limping step in his direction and . . . well, Mr. Bull got the message across to me that I should sit down and shut up, so I, uh . . .

I sat down and shut up, so to speak.

I had felt a sinking spell coming on anyway.

Just taking those two steps had worn me to a frazzle.

And also, I needed to plan my next move.

Don't you see.

All at once Slim lifted his head and let out a groan. Boy, that was good news! There for a minute, I'd thought maybe . . . but no, he was still alive. He placed the palms of his hands on the ground and pushed himself up to a kneeling position.

Good heavens, I hardly even recognized him! His eyes and mouth had vanished, and his face had become a featureless white mask that . . .

Okay, that was mostly sand. His face had gotten mashed into the sand, see, and there for a second it had . . .

He brushed the sand off his face and let out another moan. He sat there for a moment, with his head hung down and his left hand resting on the right side of his rib cage. He blinked his eyes and looked at me.

"Well, Hank, we've got ourselves in a real jackpot here."

With great effort, I hobbled over to him and began administering special Certified Red Cross CPR licks to his face. Those Certified Licks will bring a guy around as fast as anything.

I had given him several before he pushed me away and said, "Quit." Then he turned and studied Mr. Bull, who stood between us and the pickup. He was watching our every move and appeared to be thinking bad thoughts.

"Hank," said Slim, setting his teeth against the pain, "I've messed up some ribs and maybe some more things too. I need to make it to the pickup and get back to the house. Reckon you can keep that bull off me?"

Uh . . . ME? Keep the . . . hey, I was injured pretty badly myself and I'd already learned about as much from that bull as I care to, and besides . . .

He put his hand on my head and rubbed my ears. "See, I might be messed up inside. That colt mashed me pretty bad. What do you say, can you help old Slim?"

I thought it over. Sure, I could help him.

CHAPTER NINE

This Is
the Scary Part

Holding his ribs and grinding his teeth against the pain, Slim pushed himself up. The bull was watching. He snorted and dropped his head and pawed up sand with his hoof.

Slim took a step. The bull's head shot up. I could tell by the look in his eyes and the way he held his ears that he was fixing to come a-hookin'.

Slim reached down and patted me on the neck. "Okay, son, it's time for us to find out what we're made of. See what you can do."

It would be an exaggeration to say that I went streaking into the fight. I pushed myself up and hobbled out into the empty space between Slim and the bull. I glared at him and he glared at me. I raised the hair on my back, stiffened my tail, and extended my neck so that my nose was pointing at him like an arrow. And then I unleashed a low growl.

From the pickup, I heard Drover squeak, "Hank, be careful, he might try to hurt you!"

And then Little Alfred yelled, "Beat him up, Hankie! I hope you bite the snot out of him."

Behind me, I heard Slim groan and take a step. The bull's head snapped around and his eyes locked on Slim. He had just picked his target. He took a step toward Slim, and that's when I gave him some education on cowdogs.

A lot of dogs would have barked and gone through a little warmup procedure. Not me. I figgered what we needed here was a strong and lasting impression. When you want to make an impression on a bull, you don't bark and you don't bluff and you don't talk. You merely take a death grip on his nose and hang on.

And so I rushed forward, fitted my jaws around his nose before he had time to think about it, and then I went to Maximum Crunch.

Say, Old Bully didn't like that! He snorted and bellered and started slinging his head around. Since I was pretty well attached to his nose, he was slinging me around at the same time.

I went up, I went down, I went in circles, I

bounced off the ground and bounced off his horns and bounced off that big ugly hump in his neck. And yes, all this bouncing and crashing around did take its toll on my body, but the thought of slacking my grip on his nose never entered my mind.

What DID enter my mind after several minutes of this trashing was that I might not live long enough to brag about this adventure. I was taking a terrible beating, but I knew that as long as I held on to his nose, I had a chance to survive. If he ever shook me off, then he could go to work on me with his horns, and fellers . . .

Maybe my jaws got tired. Maybe he gave his head an extra hard jerk. I don't remember. I mean, things were happening pretty fast out there. But all at once, the very worst thing that could have happened happened. He broke my hold on his nose and threw me off.

I hit the ground hard, and before I could make another move, he was there on top of me—beating me, pounding me, mauling me with those huge horns. Left! Right! Left! Right!

I squalled for help but there wasn't any help. Oh, Drover was yipping from underneath the pickup, and Little Alfred yelled for the bull to "weave my doggie awone," as I recall his words. And that was about all the help I got.

The blows hurt at first, but after a while I didn't feel much pain. With each blow from a horn, my head snapped around and I could hear a crunching sound deep inside my body, but there wasn't much pain anymore.

I felt myself slipping away into a dream, as darkness gathered around the edges of my vision. The circle of darkness grew larger, and the circle of light in the center shrank down to a tiny hole.

What I could see through that hole was what

was left of my life. I watched as it slipped away from me. I kind of hated to see it go, but this was the way I'd always wanted it to be. I'd always wanted to go out fighting for my ranch.

Just before the light went out for the last time, I got some help from an unexpected source. While all this had been going on, that colt hadn't moved a muscle. He'd stood nearby, shivering and watching all the bloodshed with his big moon eyes.

Well, all at once something must have spooked him, because he took off running and bucking, and when he hit the end of that rope, he did get Mr. Bull's full attention. It jerked both of them down on the ground.

Bully didn't like that even a little bit, and when he got to his feet, he'd already decided to eat him a colt for supper. He dropped his head and charged. The colt screamed, jumped to his feet, and started hauling the mail.

Say, that was something to see, those two heavy-weights tied together on the same piece of string. First the bull jerked down the colt, then the colt jerked down the bull. Then they both went down.

I mean, it looked like total disaster there for a while, but then they jerked the horn plumb out of Slim's saddle. That nylon rope was stretched like a rubber band, and when the horn pulled out, it flew back and whopped old Bully right between the eyes.

And all at once it was over. The bull staggered away with blood dripping out of his nose. The colt bucked a few more times and nickered, and then he went to the trailer and stood there. And the dust that had filled the air began to settle around us.

Dust and silence.

Next thing I knew, Drover and Little Alfred were there beside me. Tears and dust had streaked the boy's face. He went down on his knees and threw his arms around me and hugged me a whole bunch harder than I wanted to be hugged right then.

It hurt and I yelped.

"Hankie, get up. We have to take Swim home." I tried to stand up but couldn't do it. "Huuwy, get up! We have to go home." I tried it again. Couldn't do it. "All wight, I'll have to pick you up."

He tried to carry me to the pickup but that didn't work. He just wasn't stout enough, and even if he had been, I couldn't have stood the pain.

Just then we heard Slim's voice. He had managed to crawl into the cab of the pickup and was sitting on the passenger's side, with his head propped up on his hand.

"Button, come here." The boy went over to the pickup. That left me alone with Mister Day-Late-and-Dollar-Short.

"Gosh, Hank, are you hurt pretty bad?"

"As bad as I need to be, thanks."

"You're welcome. I sure meant to come out and help you, but when that bull . . . did you see how big and ugly he was?"

"No, I wasn't close enough to get a good look at him, Drover. Was he pretty big and ugly?"

"He was terrible, just terrible! I came out to help you, honest I did, but then he . . . I just . . . oh Hank, I feel so guilty! I don't know if I can stand myself anymore!"

"You'll find a way, Drover. I've got confidence in you."

"Don't say that! Don't be nice to me, I don't deserve it. Tell me I'm worthless and chicken-hearted. Tell me I'm a failure. Tell me I should stand in the corner for the rest of my life."

"I would, son, but it hurts to talk."

"Oh, this guilt is more than I can stand! You can't believe how much it hurts me to see you hurt. If there's anything I can do, Hank, anything at all, just tell me."

"Okay, be quiet. I want to hear how Slim's going to get us out of this mess."

"Sure, Hank, just anything. I'll be quiet, but I want you to know that . . ."

"Hush."

He hushed and I listened to what Slim was saying.

"Button, here's what's got to be done. We've got to get me home and I can't drive. If I put the pickup in Grandma Low, reckon you can steer it back home?"

"Me, dwive the pickup? I don't think so, Swim."

"Sure you can. You did it coming up here. Just keep it in the road, that's all, and if anything goes wrong, turn off the key."

"Well, maybe. I can twy."

"Good boy. Now, I want you to walk over to that colt, real quiet and slow, and catch his reins. Then lead him over here as close to the pickup door as you can."

"But Swim . . ."

"Don't be scared, Button. He was acting crazy because that bull was trying to hurt him. He'll be all right. Just be smooth and don't make any sudden moves. Talk gentle to him. Go on."

Alfred looked pretty scared when he walked up to the colt, but he did just as Slim told him. The colt's eyes got big when he saw the kid coming toward him, and he had rollers in his nose, but he stood his ground. Alfred caught the reins and led him over to the pickup.

Slim reached out the window and unbuckled

the cinches: back cinch, front cinch, and breast collar. "Button, there's one more buckle and I can't reach it. It's under his chest, where the breast collar hooks into the front cinch. You'll have to get it."

Slim held the reins and talked to the horse while Alfred reached under and unbuckled the strap. "Good boy. Now, step back. I'm going to turn him a-loose."

Slim unhooked the throat latch and slipped the bridle off the colt's head. As the colt turned to leave, Slim grabbed the saddle and let it fall to the ground.

The effort of doing all that seemed to wear him out. He leaned his head back against the cab and closed his eyes for a moment. Then he said, "Let's go, Button."

"What about Hankie?"

"For now, we'll have to leave him. I hate it as much as you do, but we've got no choice."

HUH?

Leave me alone in that big lonesome pasture? Holy smokes, night would be coming in a few hours and hungry coyotes would be out looking for a meal, and *they were going to drive off and leave me there?*

CHAPTER TEN

A Buzzard Falls
Out of the Sky

Was this my reward for saving Slim from the bull? Was this the kind of thanks they gave a dog for putting his life on the line and fighting for his ranch?

Use him up and then leave him for coyote bait?

Yes, I couldn't help feeling a little bitter about it. I mean, I had only one life and one body and it seemed to me they were being a little careless with it.

But on the other hand, what else could they do? I had tried to walk and couldn't. Slim was hurt and couldn't lift me into the pickup. Alfred had tried. And Drover...

"Oh Hank, we're going to leave you out here

all alone, and boy, you talk about heavy guilt! This just might do me in."

"Drover, I've got a suggestion."

"Anything, Hank, anything at all. You just tell me what I can do."

"All right. Why don't you stay out here and keep me company?"

There for a second, I thought his eyes were going to pop out of his head. "Stay . . . keep you . . ." He started backing away. "You know, Hank, I'd love to do that, I really would, but with this leg the way it is, I sure think I'd better . . . and I wouldn't feel right about leaving headquarters without a dog to take care of things, and maybe I'd better . . ."

He turned and limped back to the pickup. "Thanks a bunch, Drover, and the next time you need my help, I hope you'll call a bull!"

"Thanks, Hank. I know everything'll be all right. Oh, this guilt is terrible!"

He hopped into the back of the pickup and that was the last I saw of the little stooge.

I looked around and there was Little Alfred, standing over me. He bent down and petted me on the head.

"We have to weeve you, Hankie, but I'll come back. I pwomise, I'll come back."

He bit his lip and ran to the pickup.

Slim put the gearshift in neutral and started the motor. Then he told Alfred to step on the clutch pedal and he shifted into first gear—Grandma Low, as he called it. Alfred let out the clutch and the pickup lurched forward.

With Alfred standing up in the seat and gripping the wheel in both hands, they made a circle in the pasture and began the long, slow trip back to the house, two miles to the south. The boy waved one last good-bye, and I heard Drover say, "Oh, the guilt! Oh, my leg!"

And then they were gone.

The silence moved over me like a fog. My friends had left, the horse had left, even the cattle had left. I had never known such a lonesome feeling in all my career. About the only thing I could cling to was Little Alfred's promise that he would come back to get me.

But that wasn't much to cling to. I knew he couldn't drive in those pastures without Slim to help him.

I checked the location of the sun. Five o'clock, was my best guess, which meant that I had four hours of daylight left before darkness fell and the local cannibals began stirring around.

My whole body ached and that hot summer sun was burning me up. I put cannibals out of my mind

and fell into a sleep—and dreamed about cannibals, dozens of them, howling and circling in the
darkness and closing in on me.

I awoke and saw that the sun had slipped
almost to the horizon. I had slept for several hours.
I glanced off to the south, hoping to see a plume
of dust in the air that would tell me that help was
on the way.

There was no plume of dust. Help was not on
the way.

My mouth was burning up with thirst, and I
began to wonder if I could drag myself over to the
stock tank and get a drink. I did a quick scan of
my bodily parts and discovered, to my surprise,
that all four legs appeared to be attached, and
even unbroken.

I'm sure the Hooking Bull would have been
disappointed to find out that after all his attempts
to shred me up like so much paper, he hadn't even
busted a leg.

Well, if I still had four unbroken legs, maybe I
could stand on them. I lifted my hind end, lifted
my front end, and found myself standing on all
four legs. I took a step.

Now, those legs were a tad wobbly and I fell
down a couple of times, and yes, the old body was
beat up and sore, but I finally managed to limp

and weave my way to the stock tank.

The next challenge came when I tried to stand on my hind legs, lean over the edge of the tank, and lap up some of that nice, sweet, cool windmill water. It was tough, let me tell you, but once I got the smell of that water, I didn't quit until I had lapped up a bellyful.

And once I had gone that far, I began to wonder if maybe I could pull myself over the edge of the tank and take a little dip. I hopped and I pulled and I tugged, and every one of those bruised muscles talked to me, but by George I made it up to the edge and let myself tumble over into the water

Oh, that was the most wonderful feeling! I was surrounded by cool friendly water, and I found swimming quite a bit easier on my injured parts than walking. It was very nice, paddling around in that nice cool water.

Only trouble was that when I tried to climb out, I couldn't. Seems that the the water in my hair had increased my weight just enough so that I, well, couldn't get out. I swam another lap and tried it again. Same deal.

My first thought was that I would probably drown, but then I realized that by placing my hind feet on the bottom of the tank and hanging my front paws over the edge, I could stand up. That was a welcome discovery, because drowning in a stock tank just didn't fit into my plans at all.

Well, there I was, more or less stranded in a tank of water, when I heard a flapping sound in the air above me. This was followed a moment later by a metallic "ping" and a noise that I can only describe as a loud squawk, something like this: "Awk, awk, awk!"

Then something large and black and ugly hit the water with a big kersplash. Kind of startled me. Well, you know me. When things fall out of the sky and land in the water only a few feet away, I don't just stand there. I bark!

Yes sir, I barked. Since I was injured, it wasn't my usual deep ferocious bark, but it wasn't all that bad either. I had a feeling that whatever had fallen into the tank would get the message.

Well, the subject . . . creature, thing, whatever it was, came up sputtering and flapping its . . . hmmm, flapping its wings. That was my first clue. No, actually the second. The first clue, now that I began to focus my powers of concentration, had been "big and black and ugly." To that information I added the "flapping of wings," and bingo, I had sketched out the identity of the mysterious intruder.

We had us a buzzard in the stock tank, is what

we had. Now all that remained was for me to determine which of the two local buzzards had been dumb enough to fall off the windmill tower.

"Halt! Who goes there! State your name, rank, and brand of cereal at once!"

"Shut up, dog, you're supposed to be our supper and I'm a-fixing to drown if I don't get out of here. Junior, you git yourself down here and save my life, it was you that pushed me into that dadgummed windmill fan and got me knocked off the dadgummed tower!"

"W-w-w-well, y-you k-kept c-c-c-crowdin' me and y-you sh-shouldn't be so p-p-pushy all the t-t-time, all the time. Y-y-you're s-so g-g-g-g-greedy, it s-s-serves you r-r-right."

"That's a fine thang for a boy to say about his own flesh and blood, his poor old daddy who's scrimped and saved and tried to bring him up right!"

"W-w-when did y-you s-s-scrimp and s-s-s-save?"

By this time the pieces of the puzzle had fallen into place. What we had was a buzzard named Wallace in the stock tank and another named Junior up on the windmill tower.

There was a moment of silence, so I took the opportunity to say, "Excuse me, but it seems to me . . ."

"Shut up, dog, this here's a family affair and we

don't need your two cents." He turned back to Junior. "When did I scrimp and save? Son, I've scrimped and saved a thousand times over the years as I tried to teach you right from wrong, and how to get along in a hostile world."

"Y-y-yeah, but I m-m-mean l-lately."

"Lately? All right, maybe I've backslid a little and maybe I haven't scrimped and saved as much I should have, but that don't mean . . . son, I'm a-fixing to drown, buzzards wasn't built for swimming!"

"M-m-maybe our d-d-doggie f-f-friend will he-he-help you. H-hi, d-d-doggie."

I dipped my head at him. "How's it going, Junior?"

"Oh f-f-f-fine, except P-p-pa's f-fixing to, uh, d-d-drown to d-d-death in the w-w-w-w-w-w . . . stock t-t-tank."

"Well, I could probably help the old wretch, if he'd just show the courtesy of asking for it."

Wallace thrashed and sputtered. "Forget that, pooch! I ain't a rich bird and I ain't got much to show for all these years of toil and woe, but I've got my pride, yes I do, and I have never accepted help from my supper!"

I shrugged. "In that case, I hope you enjoy drowning as much as I'll enjoying letting you."

At this point you're probably sitting on the edge of your chair, wondering if I actually let the old buzzard drown.

Yes, I did.

Or let's put it this way. To find out if Wallace drowned, and if I was eaten by hungry cannibals, you'll have to keep on reading and go to the next chapter.

I'm out of room for this chapter, see.

A Buzzard
Family Feud

O kay, we had one buzzard drowning in the stock tank and another buzzard perched on top of the windmill tower. Pretty exciting, huh?

I lifted my head and spoke to Junior, up on the tower. "I've done all a dog can do, Junior. I guess you're about to become an orphan."

"Oh d-d-d-darn. H-he's so s-s-s-stubborn. And g-g-g-greedy."

"Help! Son, is that all you can say after all I've done for you, after all the wonderful times we've enjoyed together? Just think of all the many dead skunks we've shared."

"Y-y-yeah, b-but y-you always g-g-g-g-got the s-s-skunk and I g-got the s-s-s-stink."

"No, I never, sometimes you say the most hateful things, Junior, I cain't imagine where you come up with 'em, but the point is that I am a-fixing to DROWN!"

Junior didn't say another word. Neither did I. We just watched as the old man thrashed and squawked and sputtered. His ugly bald head went under two times, and that second trip seemed to have made an impression on him.

"Say there, neighbor, I don't reckon you could spare the time to help a poor old buzzard who's down on his luck, could you now?"

"Oh, I might. Do you suppose that poor old buzzard could say please?"

"NO, I CERTAIN DON'T THINK..." His head went under again. "Yes, by crackies, I sure think we could...dog, would you please grab a-holt of me and spare me from this fate of drowning to death?"

I dog-paddled out to where he was and offered him a paw. He took the paw AND the leg, climbed up on top of my head, pushed me underwater, and hopped up on the rim of the tank. When I came up, he was sitting there, dripping water and glaring at me and the rest of the world.

"That's what you git for tryin' to force manners on a buzzard. It ain't natural."

"Does that mean the same as 'thank you'?"

"No, it sure don't. I ain't sayin' thank you to no pot-lickin' ranch dog, and in fact, I'm a-takin' back the 'please' I just said."

Junior almost fell off the tower when he heard that. "Y-y-y-you c-c-can't d-do th-that, P-p-p-pa. Y-you c-c-can't t-t-take b-back p-p-pleases, once y-you've s-s-s-said 'em."

Wallace glared up at him. "Who says I cain't? If I gave it, I can take it back. If I said it, I can un-say it. If I offered it in the spirit of brotherhood,

I can unoffer it in the spirit of true Buzzard-hood."

"B-b-but P-pa, he s-s-saved your l-l-life!"

"So? He done the world a huge favor and that ort to be reward enough in itself, and he don't need me sayin' a bunch of mealymouth thank-yous that I don't believe in, and which no buzzard worth shootin' would believe in, and you could take a lesson from that yourself, son, and quit carryin' on like an I-don't-know-what, and puttin' on airs, because you ain't a little humming-bird, son, you're a BUZZARD, from a long line of buzzards."

The old man turned to me. "And buzzards is buzzards, and we're proud to be buzzards, and buzzards don't say PLEASE and buzzards don't say THANK YOU, especially to dogs, and you can either put that in your pipe and smoke it, or chew it up and spit it out, I don't give a rip which."

Up on the tower, Junior gave his head a sad shake. "Oh P-p-pa, y-you're s-s-so t-terrible!"

"That's right, and proud of it too."

At that very moment—you won't believe this—at that very moment, I thought I heard music, real pretty music, and Junior started singing this song.

Family Fugue

Junior
    Sometimes, Pa, I think you are a dirty
        rotten cad.
    You're my dad,
    But still, I think you could adjust.
    You simply must acquire some polish and
        some class.

    Saying please won't hurt your reputation,
        and in fact,
    It could help you some.
    It's dumb to offend the very one
    Who's lent a hand and pulled you drowning
        from a tank.

Wallace
    Son, I've tried to school you in the facts
        of buzzard lore,
    You're a bore.
    But still, I think you could adjust.
    You really must quit talking nonsense to
        your pa.

    Buzzards by their very definition are
        uncouth,

That's the truth.
What's dumb is showing courtesy and
    manners
To the very dog we came here just to eat.

Junior
    Yeah, but Pa, I think you ought to show
        some courtesy
    Just to me.
    Because we are kinfolks doesn't mean you
        have a right
    To treat me like we're relatives.

    I can see there's very little hope of getting
        through
    To you.
    I'm glad I pushed you off the windmill
        tower
    And I hope that almost drowning did you
        good.

Wallace (counter melody)
    This boy talks nonsense.
    Where did I fail?
    Where did I go wrong?
    He didn't learn it from his pa.

I won't say thank you.

I won't say please.

I will ignore you.

And I hope that this ignoring does you good.

When they were done with the song, the old man turned to me and said, "And that's my last word on the subject, I don't want to hear any more about it, and Junior, me and you need to be scoutin' around for something dead to eat, and if we don't hurry, it's liable to be ME."

"Y-y-yeah, I'm about to s-s-starve."

"We come here two hours ago, thinkin' this silly dog was going to be the answer to our prayers, but here he is . . ." The old man gave me the evil eye. "You're a-wasting our time, dog. Are you available for supper or ain't you? Just a simple yes or no, never mind the details."

"No."

"Fine. Junior, with one simple word, this dog has just broke my heart into thirteen pieces. I don't know what your plans are for the rest of the evening, but I'm fixin' to get airborne and hunt grub." Then back to me: "But things change, puppy, and we'll sure 'nuff check you out first thing in the morning."

And with that, he pointed himself into the

wind, pushed off the edge of the tank, flapped his wings, and climbed into the evening sky.

Junior grinned down at me from the tower. "H-h-he's j-just awful s-s-sometimes. W-well, I g-guess I'd b-b-better g-go or h-he'll be b-b-back and s-s-start y-yelling at m-me again. B-bye, D-d-doggie."

"See you around, Junior, and say, I liked that song."

"Oh th-thanks. P-pa d-didn't h-h-hear any of it, b-but I'm g-glad you l-l-l-l-liked it. B-bye."

He rocked back and forth three times, and with a loud grunt, pushed off the windmill tower and flew away. No sooner had the swish of his wings vanished in the distance than I heard another sound that sent shivers of dread down my spine.

"Ahh-ooooooo!"

Coyotes, and they were close. Holy smokes, darkness was coming and there I was, all alone in the pasture, too beat up and injured to climb out of the stock tank and run for my life!

"Ah-ooooooo! Ah-ooooooo!"

There it was again, the evening song of heartless hairy cannibals. The howls were close and coming closer. By now they had picked up my scent and were moving in for the kill. I could almost see their yellow eyes sparkling and the foam dripping off their deadly fangs.

Crouched and shivering in my watery grave, I held my breath and listened. I heard the swish of their paws in the grass. I heard them belching and laughing. Then, much to my dismay, I heard them tune up and sing the Coyote Sacred Hymn and National Anthem.

Me just a worthless coyote,
Me howling at the moon.
Me like to sing and holler,
Me crazy as a loon.

Me not want job or duties,
No church or Sunday school.
Me just a worthless coyote
But me ain't nobody's fool.

I had heard those two verses before, and indeed, in better days I had even sung them with Rip and Snort on several occasions. I had never heard them sing but the two verses and wouldn't have bet a nickel that they knew any more, but now, before my very ears, they sang a third verse.

Me catch the smell of supper,
A-floating in the breeze.

With all this dust and pollen,
It make me want to sneeze.

It smell like something yummy,
It smell like something neat.
It smell just like a HOT DOG,
And hot dog, me love to eat!

I didn't like that new verse, not at all. In fact,
it made me, uh, very nervous to hear them out
there in the darkness . . . I sure needed to get out
of that stock tank, and all my instincts began
screaming RUN! in the back of my mind.

But running from heartless hairy cannibals
was a sure and certain way to get caught. I mean,
you might as well try to run away from your own
shadow. Once those guys locked into a scent and
got on a trail, there was no stopping them, no
escape.

I didn't run. I couldn't have run, even if I'd
wanted to, and so I hunkered down in the water
and waited like a helpless rabbit—waited and
listened to the sounds of my assassins as they
came closer, ever closer.

I could make out their voices now: Rip and
Snort. I recognized the tone of their belching. Well,
maybe I could talk my way out of this. I had done

it before. Rip and Snort were heartless brutes but they had their weak spots. Maybe if...

But then I heard another voice, and all my hopes were dashed. It was a deep and cruel voice. It belonged to Scraunch the Terrible.

"Scraunch think we come to end of trail. Here at windmill, we find big yummy ranch dog, oh boy!"

And with that, Scraunch walked up to the edge of the tank and looked inside.

CHAPTER TWELVE

Saved Just in the Nick of Time

"Uh!" said Scraunch. "Not see yummy dog supper in tank. Better we look around windmill."

Heh, heh. Maybe you thought he would look inside the tank and see me there, huh? And then eat me alive? Well, that could have happened to one of your ordinary ranch dogs, but don't forget that those coyotes were dealing with the Head of Ranch Security.

I had my little bag of tricks, see. When I saw Scraunch's nose appear over the rim of the tank, I took a big gulp of air and *went underwater*. It was just dark enough by then so that he couldn't see me.

Pretty clever, huh?

When I came up for air, I heard them chasing around and yelling at each other. It really had 'em buffaloed. My scent was strong around the tank and they knew I was somewhere close by, but they couldn't find me. And the more they looked, the madder they got and the louder they yelled at each other.

Snort blamed Rip and Rip blamed Scraunch and Scraunch blamed Snort, and after a while they stopped looking for me and got into a big fight. You never heard so much snarling and carrying on.

Well, I was sitting there in the water, feeling pretty proud of myself and listening to the brawl, when I happened to notice a sharp-pointed nose appear over the rim of the tank. Uh-oh. Snort had decided to take a look around.

I took a gulp of air and slipped under the water. I stayed under as long as I could, then had to come back up. The same routine had worked on Scraunch and I felt pretty sure that . . .

I could see Snort's eyes flickering in the moonlight. He was looking straight at me. "Uh! What that swimming around in tank?"

"Quack, quack," I said.

I could hear his nose testing for scent. "Uh! That goose in there?"

"Quack."

"Sound more like duck in there."

"Quack."

"Sound like duck but smell like dog. Not make sense."

"Quack, quack."

"Uh. Sound like pretty stupid duck."

"Quack."

"Duck not say quack just like that. Duck have different kind of quack."

"Quack."

"Sound berry more like DOG quack than duck quack."

"Quack, quack, quack." He was sniffing the air again, and I began to worry.

"Ah ha! Snort solve mystery of stupid duck! Stupid duck not stupid duck at all."

"Quack?"

"Stupid duck really Hunk dog trying hide in water! And coyote plenty mad for stupid duck-trick in water."

I had been exposed. "Now hold on just a minute, Snort, I can explain everything."

"Snort not give hoot for explain everything."

"I was just taking a bath, see, taking a normal everyday kind of bath, and thought it might be fun to, uh, play ducks." Two more coyote heads appeared over the rim of the tank. "Well, by George, look who's . . . I was just telling old Snort . . . I'll admit it sounds strange, a grown dog playing ducks in a stock tank, but if you'll hear me out, I'm sure you'll agree . . ."

Scraunch ran his tongue over both sides of his mouth, a real bad sign. "Time for big eat. Hunk get out or coyote get in?"

I studied the faces before me—the gleaming eyes, the gleaming fangs, the hungry looks. "So this is it, is that what you're saying?" Three heads nodded. "There's no chance that we could work this out on paper?" All three shook their heads. "In that case, boys, you'd better come and get it, 'cause there's no free lunch on this ranch!"

I swam to the middle of the tank and prepared to make my last stand. The coyotes yipped and hollered, and Scraunch came diving over the side.

"Scraunch, it's only fair that I tell you that I'm a black belt in Water Karate." He kept coming toward me. "Listen, that deal with the duck was only a joke, honest." He kept coming. "It's still not too late to . . ."

Before I could finish my sentence, he sprang at me, clamped his powerful jaws around the scruff of my neck, and plunged my head under the . . . blub, blub.

Gurgle, blub, gargle, blubber.

. . . water.

I had just about checked out of this old world when . . . that was odd, Scraunch released his death grip on my neck and . . . let me come up for air? That didn't make any sense, unless he wanted the fight to go more than one round.

But whatever, I accepted the offer and came up gasping for air, just in time to see three coyotes drag their dripping selves over the side of the tank. They ran through the beam of two headlights and vanished into the night.

Headlights? I hadn't noticed any . . . holy smokes, somebody had come to my rescue! Or was I dreaming?

I heard a car door open and close. Then . . . Little Alfred's voice! "Hankie, here Hankie! I came back for you. Where are you?"

Hey, I barked, I howled, I moaned, I whined, and then I struck out swimming for the edge of the tank. When I got there, I was pulled out by Little Alfred and, I'll be derned, Miss Viola, Slim's lady friend.

And yes, Mister Burden-of-Guilt was there, hopping up and down and spinning around in circles. "Oh my gosh, Hank, when we didn't see you, we thought maybe the coyotes had got you, and boy, you talk about feeling bad about something! I wasn't sure I could make it through the night."

"Thanks, Drover. In the absence of meaningful action, it's the thought that counts."

"You bet, and boy, I've done lots of thinking, sure have."

Well, Miss Viola picked me up and carried me to Slim's pickup and laid me on the floorboard (I was still wet, see). And on the way back to the ranch, I began piecing together the rest of the story.

After they had left me at the windmill, Slim and Little Alfred made the slow drive back to headquarters, with the boy at the controls and the pickup in Grandma Low. When they got there, Slim crawled on his hands and knees into the house and called Miss Viola on the phone.

She lived down the creek, you might recall, about five miles below our place, and she came streaking up the valley to take care of Slim. She tried to load him up in her car and take him to the doctor, but he didn't have any great love for doctors or hospitals, and anyways, by that time he'd already diagnosed his own case.

He'd been mashed pretty badly by that horse, but the wreck had taken place in soft sand, so he'd come out of it with some bruises and cracked ribs—just the kind of things he could treat with wool fat, salty meat grease, and Absorbine Jr. And no doctor.

So Miss Viola got him loaded into a bed and sent Little Alfred down to the saddle shed for all that high-tech medicine, and after a couple of hours, old Slim was back on the road to recovery.

And it was then that Little Alfred remembered his promise to me and coaxed Miss Viola into driving up into the pasture to get me. So there you are.

When we got back to headquarters, Miss Viola carried me into the house and made a pallet for me on the floor beside Slim's bed. They discussed the pros and cons of letting me stay in Sally May's house, but they decided that since I had saved Slim from the Hooking Bull and had shown incredible courage on the field of battle, it was only right that I should be allowed to stay inside.

Which was plenty fine with me. As beat-up as I was, the thought of camping out on my gunny-sack bed didn't excite me much.

And let me tell you, before she went back home that night, Miss Viola made quite a fuss over me and my injuries. She pulled all the burs, moss, and mud out of my coat. She dug a few ticks out of my ears and gave me a good brushing. And what would you say if I told you she fixed me some warm milk with a raw egg mixed in?

Honest, she did all that. Miss Viola not only had good taste in dogs, but she knew how to make invalidism pretty derned attractive. I mean, I could have stood quite a lot of that kind of treatment.

The next morning she came back and fixed us guys a nice big breakfast. Would you believe scrambled eggs and bacon for ME? Shucks, I made up my mind right then that if Slim didn't have sense enough to marry that gal, I just might give it a shot myself.

Well, everything was just about perfect, right up to the moment we heard the car pull up in front of the house. It was Loper and Sally May, back from their trip, and suddenly I began feeling very uneasy about, well, being in Sally May's house, for one thing, but then there was another little matter that, uh, weighed even heavier on my mind.

It had to do with strawberry ice cream.

Sally May was not overjoyed to see me inside the house. I could tell by the way her nostrils flared and her eyes widened. But Miss Viola handled it very well. She explained that I had saved Slim from being made into sausage by the Hooking Bull, and that she, Viola, had taken it upon herself to let me stay inside.

By George, it worked! Sally May loosened up, smiled a little bit, and even came over and gave me several kind words and pats on the head.

After all the hard times and misunderstandings Sally May and I had gone through, this was major victory, but still, I couldn't enjoy it. I kept wondering what form of execution she would choose for me when she found . . . well, the strawberry ice cream.

But you know what? Just at the time when I was about to have a nervous breakthrough, Miss Viola came over to my bed, bent down, and whispered, "Don't worry, I cleaned it up."

What a woman! What an angel! I survived the day in grand style and lived happily ever after.

Oh, were you wondering what happened to the Hooking Bull? Three days later, Slim was back on his feet and, shall we say, thirsting for revenge. He and Loper saddled the two stoutest horses on the ranch and went up to the north pasture.

I'm told that to this very day, you can see deep skid marks all the way from the windmill to the gate in the northeast corner of the pasture. The Hooking Bull got invited to a sledding party, and we haven't seen him since.

Case closed.

Have you read all
of Hank's adventures?

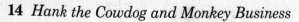

Join H...
the C... 's
Se...

Are yo...
you'll ...
Here i...

Welco
- A
- F

Eight
- S
- L
- Sp
- F

More
- Sp
- A
- U
  w

Total ... 95.
Howe...
shippi...

☐ Yes
($8.95
ship.

WHIC
CHOO

YOUR

MAILI

CITY

TELEP   an?

E-MAIL

Sen

Han
Mav   D.
P.O.   y.
Perr

*The H...   sole
respon...   in*
Putnam Inc., Puffin Books, Viking Children's Books, or their subsidiaries or affiliates.